Red and I Visit the Vet

Written by Mindy Menschell
Illustrated by Bruce Armstrong

Silver Burdett Ginn
A Division of Simon & Schuster
160 Gould Street
Needham Heights, MA 02194-2310

Design and production by Kirchoff/Wohlberg, Inc.

ISBN 0-663-59375-1

2 3 4 5 6 7 8 9 10 SP 01 00 99 98 97 96

Today we need to take Red to see
the vet.

3

The vet's name is Dr. Chen.

She asks Red a lot of questions. But Red is shy. So I have to answer for him.

5

Dr. Chen looks in Red's mouth.

"Red, how are your teeth?" she asks.

Red does not answer. So I do.

"I help Red keep his teeth clean."

Dr. Chen checks Red's nose.

"Red, how is your nose?" she asks.

Red does not answer. So I do.

"His nose is always cold and wet."

Dr. Chen listens to Red's chest.

"So Red, how's that old chest today?"
she asks.

Red and I are quiet so Dr. Chen can listen.

Dr. Chen needs to check Red's feet.

"How are your feet today?" she asks.

Red does not answer. So I do.

"His feet always get him where he wants to go."

"Your pet seems very healthy," says
Dr. Chen. "Keep taking good care of
your pet.

14

Feed him and give him water. And he
needs a walk every day, rain or shine."

"Red, you passed your checkup. How do you feel now?"

This time Red does answer. He wags his tail.

I just smile.